FIVE YEARS AGO...

ISBN# 978-1-329-58253-8

BLOOD GAMES is published by Five Strangers Press. First Printing. A division of Five Strangers Films LLC. 600 E Olive Avenue #310, Burbank, CA 91501. www.fivestrangersfilms.com. The stories, incidents, names, characters and places are ficticious and a product of the author's imagination. Any similarities to any persons real or dead are purely coincidental. Copyright 2003 - 2015 by Five Strangers Films LLC. This edition is published by Five Strangers Comics. Copyright 2015. All rights reserved. No part of this book may be transmitted in any form or by any means electronic or mechanical, including photocopying, recording or by any information storage or retrieval system, withour the written permission of the publisher, except where permitted by law. Printed and published in the USA.

THE LONG HALLWAY COMES TO A DEAD END.

THE SOUNDS OF FEASTING STOP.

AHHHHH!!!!!

THELONIUS VON RHYLOS, THE HEAD VAMPIRE. THE ONE TO FEAR AND HATE.

AS PETER FALTERS, OUT OF THIN AIR, A OMINOUS FIGURE APPREARS.

MR. CHURCH I OFFER YOU A PROPOSITION. YOU CAN STILL GET OUT OF THIS GAME.

GOD SAVE ME!

INTERESTING THAT AT THE POINT OF DEATH, PEOPLE FIND GOD.

GO TO HELL!

PETER'S SCREAM WILL FALL UPON DEAF EARS.

WHAT'S WRONG WITH HIM?

AS THE GROUP TRIES TO COMPREHEND THIS IMPOSSIBLE SITUATION, THEY GATHER OVER THE UNCONSCIOUS PETER.

"HE'S INSANE!"

FROM THIN AIR, APPEARS THE CRIMINAL WHO'S THE CAUSE OF THEIR ANGST.

THELONIUS VON RHYLOS.

THE GROUP SCATTERS AT THE UNFAMILIAR VOICE.

THE GROUP LOOKS UP, FRIGHTENED BY THE STEELY EYES OF THE VICIOUS STRANGER.

WHAT'S YOUR **DAMAGE?**

THEY DECIDE THAT ANSWERS ARE BETTER THAN FOOD.

BEFORE WE BEGIN, FINISH EATING.

MR. JOBIDAN, YOU NEED TO LEARN SOME RESPECT.

BLOW ME. WHERE'S MY WATCH?

PERHAPS I SHOULD CLARIFY. YOU ARE CARRYING PETER CHURCH.

HE'S THE ONE WHO OFFENDED ME THE LEAST.

PETER CHURCH? HE'S A HIGH PROFILE CRIMINAL ATTORNEY.

YOU KNOW HIM?

HE'S BEEN MISSING FOR ABOUT FIVE YEARS.

THERE WERE OTHERS...

THEY'RE DEAD.

"IMPOSSIBLE."

"I AM A VAMPIRE."

"BUT DR. VERA NICHOLS ALREADY KNOWS THAT."

"YOU SHALL USE EACH OTHER'S WITS AND SKILLS TO NEGOTIATE MY LAIR. SHOULD ANYONE MAKE IT OUT ALIVE THEY WILL RECEIVE MY ENTIRE FORTUNE."

"ALRIGHT, **THAT'S IT**..."

"I SAY WE **TEACH CAKE-BOY** HERE, THE MEANING OF **PAIN**."

NYUHHHH!!!

RHYLOS HAS NO PATIENCE FOR THE BACK-TALK OF THE INSECTS THAT HE CHOOSES FOR HIS GAMES.

HE GRABS THE INSOLENT'S NECK AND CHOKES HIM, MORE THAN PREPARED TO END THIS PEON'S LIFE.

"**STOP IT,** YOU'RE **HURTING** HIM!"

JANET HESITATES FOR THE LONGEST TIME, THEN FINALLY...

I'M A **COP**

THE **LAST** THING I NEED IS TO BE STUCK IN A **ROOM** WITH A **DAMN PIG**.

IT'S THIS **PIG** THAT'S **TRYING** TO GET YOU **OUT OF HERE**.

SHIV BRINGS IT.

YOU BETTER GET OUT OF MY FACE.

MAKE ME.

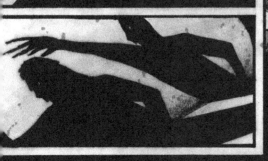

BACK IN THE PREVIOUS ROOM.

THE VAMPIRES GATHER AS RHYLOS SURVEYS THE GAME.

THEY ARE SMARTER THAN MOST.

WE'LL HAVE A GAME YET.

"CAN WE REST? IT'S BEEN AN HOUR."

TIRED, WEARY AND EXHAUSTED, THEIR ANGER IS ONLY SUPERSEDED BY THEIR FATIGUE.

THE OTHERS SURVEY THE SITUATION. PERHAPS SAVING THEIR STRENGTH IS A GOOD IDEA.

"TELL ME ABOUT THESE THINGS."

"THEY AREN'T VAMPIRES. THEY ARE VERY SICK PEOPLE WHO HAVE A DISEASE."

"WHAT KIND OF DISEASE?"

"PORPHYRIA. IT'S A LACK OF HEME IN YOUR BLOOD CELLS."

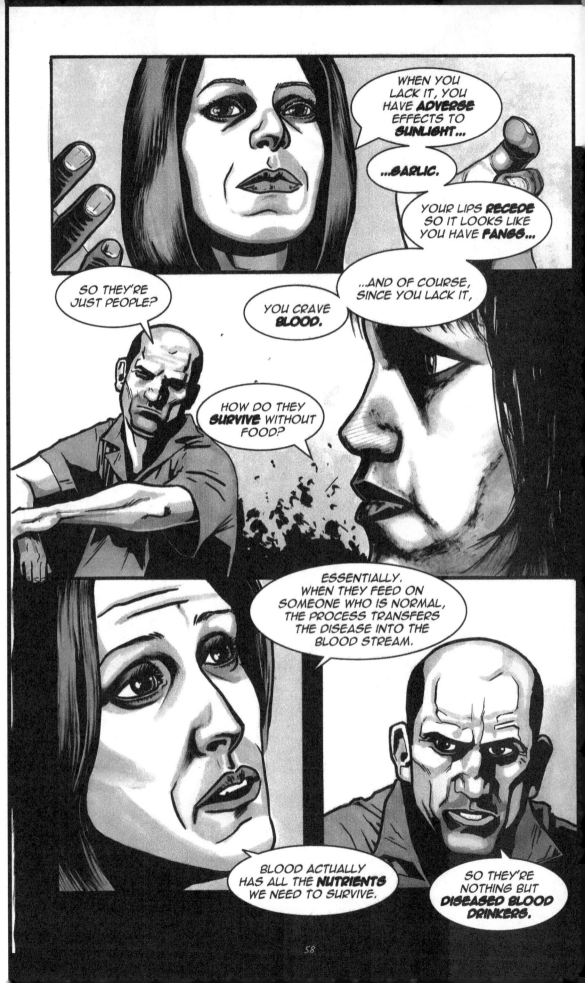

"WHY WOULD A VAMPIRE HAVE FAITH IN GOD?"

"MAYBE HE'S SEEN THE DEVIL."

PETER STARTS TO CONVULSE.

COUGHING UP BLOOD

THIS IS DIFFERENT THAN BEFORE.

"WHAT NOW?"

"I THINK HE CAN SENSE THEM."

"WE HAVE TO GET HIM TO A DOCTOR."

THE FAINT SOUND OF GROWLING AND RUNNING FEET START GET CLOSER.

"ARE THEY COMING?"

"I CAN'T HEAR ANYTHING."

THEY ATTACK.

BEFORE THE NEXT THOUGHT.

I'VE STABBED THIS ONE ALREADY!

INSTINCTS TAKE OVER.

THESE WERE ONCE PEOPLE.

SISTERS, MOTHERS... DAUGHTERS.

FATHERS, SONS.

NOW, ALL UNDEAD VAMPIRES, WANTING TO TAKE LIFE.

I DON'T KNOW HOW MUCH LONGER I CAN HOLD OUT.

BRIAN HOLDS THEM BACK AS LONG AS HE CAN.

WILL WE NOW BECOME THEM?

PETER HAS BEEN HERE BEFORE.

HE KNOWS THE PAIN.

I CAN'T TRUST YOU.

NO, NO MORE.

RHYLOS' TEETH DIG INTO THE SOFT FLESH OF PETER CHURCH.

ONLY THE SOUNDS OF PENETRATED FLESH...

...AND THE GURGLE OF BLOOD REMAIN.

IT'LL BE ALRIGHT.

EVERYTHING WILL BE FINE.

THE GIRL DROPS.

CHUCK FIRING HIS GUN CAUSES A CHAIN REACTION.

BLAM!

THE DEALERS PULL THEIR GUNS AND FIRE.

BLAM! BLAM! BLAM!

CHUCK IS SHOT.

THE CONNECTION ESCAPES OUT THE BACK WAY.

JANET, WITNESSING HER PARTNER DIE IN FRONT OF HER TRIES HER BEST TO KEEP HER FACULTIES.

BLAM! BLAM!

AT LEAST UNTIL THEY ARE ALL DEAD, OR SHE WILL BE NEXT IN LINE.

"MARCEL."

"SAM, WHAT WAS HIS NAME?"

JANET FILES THE NAME 'MARCEL' IN HER MEMORY AS THEY TRAVEL TO THE NEXT ROOM.

TEMPERANCE

WHERE THEY DISCOVER SOMEONE VERY FAMILIAR.

VERA RUSHES TO HIS AIDE.

"HE'S JUST BEEN BIT."

WHILE THE OTHERS TRY TO DECIPHER THE WORD.

"JUSTICE AND FORTITUDE."

"TEMPERANCE?"

"IT'S ONE OF THE SEVEN **HEAVENLY VIRTUES**."

"FAITH, HOPE, CHARITY, PRUDENCE, TEMPERANCE... UH."

"SHOCKED THAT A **CRIMINAL** KNOWS THE BIBLE?"

PETER RUNS SCREAMING BACK TO THE ROOM.

THWACK!

Ahhhhhhhhh!!!!!

ONLY TO GET AN PUNCH IN THE FACE FROM SHIV.

THE LANDING IMPALES PETER FROM BEHIND.

THUD

Shook!

AHHHH, THE PAIN!

WAIT, WAIT. I KNOW THIS GUY.

ARE YOU SURE?

I SET UP THE DEAL WITH THIS GUY.

I DIDN'T RECOGNIZE HIM AT FIRST, BUT **THIS IS THE GUY!**

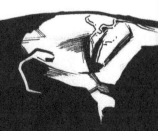

MITCH JUST RUNS WITH ALL HIS MIGHT, FORGETTING HE'S WITHIN A MAZE.

VERA IS CLOSE BEHIND. NEVER HAS SHE RUN SO HARD IN HER LIFE.

BRIAN RUNS DOWN THE SAME HALLWAY BUT VERA'S ALREADY GONE.

HE TURNS LEFT AND RIGHT DOWN HALLWAYS.

HE'S LOST.

SHIV, NOT CONCERNED ABOUT ANYONE ELSE'S SAFETY, RUNS AWAY FROM THE GROWLING.

WHEREAS JANET TRIES TO FIND THE OTHERS.

PETER. POOR PETER.

THE LAST THING THEY NEED IS TO BE SEPARATED.

I TRIED TO SAVE YOU, I SWEAR I TRIED.

SHIV - ALONE IN THE MAZE FINDS AN EMPTY ROOM.

ALMOST EMPTY.

YOU BRO.

WHERE HAVE YOU BEEN MAN?

JUSTICE

MARCEL?

BROTHERS REUNITED.

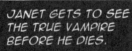

I JUST WANTED TO MAKE BUILDINGS.

YOU SAID NOTHING WOULD HAPPEN TO ME.

HOW COULD I KNOW?

HE'S NOW A MONSTER.

MARCEL TURNS AROUND AND HE'S NOT THE BROTHER SHIV ONCE HAD.

SNARL

SHIV STRUGGLES WITH THE VAMPIRE MARCEL.

UNTIL HE FINALLY GETS THE UPPER HAND...

AHHH!!

...AND THlROWS HIM TO THE GROUND.

HI DADDY.

SWEETHEART?

DADDY, THE POLICE WERE HERE.

IT SEEMS LIKE JUST YESTERDAY WHEN BRIAN TOOK NICOLE TO UNIVERSITY.

HAVE YOU FINISHED PACKING?

DADDY, WHAT DID THEY WANT?

THEY HAD TO ASK ME A FEW QUESTIONS.

THEY SAID THAT YOU KNEW VITO SABATINO.

BRIAN COULD NEVER LIE TO HIS DAUGHTER.

MITCH SILENTLY PRAYS FOR HIS LIFE.

MR. JOBIDAN.

CRAP.

IF THE SITUATION COULD HAVE GOTTEN WORSE, — IT JUST DID.

YOU'VE BEEN A VERY BAD MAN MR. JOBIDAN...

...RIGGING THE COURT SYSTEM...

....FREEING CONFESSED CRIMINALS.

I NEVER DID ANYTHING ILLEGAL.

JURY TAMPERING, WITHHOLDING EVIDENCE, WITNESS BRIBING.

OH, **THAT** ILLEGAL.

GIVEN MY CURRENT SITUATION, I DON'T THINK HE'S LISTENING.

YOU ARE AN UNUSUAL ONE. USUALLY AT THIS POINT PEOPLE FIND GOD.

ENOUGH.

JANET IS UNSURE THE EXACT REASON SHE SHOT MITCH.

BLAM!

PLOK

WAS IT BECAUSE SHE JUST COULDN'T FATHOM THE GAME CONTINUING WITH A WHOLE NEW SET OF PEOPLE.

OR WAS IT BECAUSE HE DESERVED A BULLET IN THE HEAD.

BLAM!

ANOTHER WILL PUT RHYLOS IN HIS PLACE.

BLAM!

THE BULLETS IMPACT, BUT NOT WITH THE EFFECT SHE THOUGHT.

RHYLOS SHAKES OFF THE WOUNDS AND ORDERS THE SUCCUBI TO ATTACK!

FORTITUDE

WITH A BEVY OF VAMPIRES CHASING HER, JANET SCURRIES WITH ALL HER MIGHT TO THE NEXT ROOM.

SHE MEETS UP WITH SHIV, HAVING JUST COME FROM HIS OWN EXPERIENCE.

CRAP! LOCKED DOOR!

THE ONLY WAY IS DOWN THE HALLWAY WITH THE LOCKED DOOR.

WHERE'S YOU GET THAT?

IT WAS ALL A SET-UP RIGHT FROM THE BEGINNING.

YOUR BROTHER, THE DEAL, EVERYTHING.

WE WEREN'T MEANT TO MAKE IT BACK.

POW!

WE HAVE TO GET OUT OF HERE.

WITH THE VAMPIRES CLOSE BEHIND. THEY RUN WITH ALL THEIR MIGHT.

SHIV IS RUNNING, BUT KNOWS TO NO END.

JANET.

HE KNOWS IT'S ONLY SECONDS BEFORE THEY ARE AFTER HIM AGAIN.

HE STARES AT THE DEAD END WALL.

ONE BULLET LEFT.

HE ALWAYS FIGURED HE'D DIE FROM A BULLET, BUT NEVER LIKE THIS.

"THEY'RE WEAK. I WAS TAKING OUT LIKE THIRTY OF THEM AT ONCE..."

JANET STEADIES HERSELF...

...FOR NOW SHE'S WEAK.

GASP!

THE VAMPIRES SWARM TAKING DOWN JANET.

SHIV MAKES IT THROUGH KNOWING THAT JUST ON THE OTHER SIDE OF THAT WALL IS CERTAIN DEATH.

THE FINAL ROOM.

I DID IT.

CHARITY

THE ONLY THING BETWEEN HIM AND FREEDOM...

THE GAME ISN'T OVER YET.

A 250 YEAR-OLD ANGRY VAMPIRE.

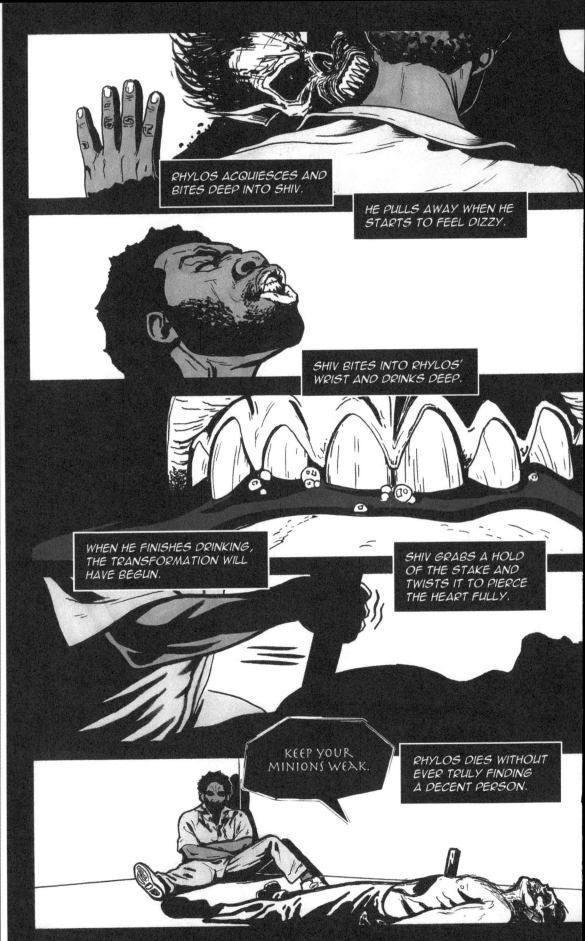

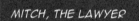

"IF WE KILL THE HEAD VAMPIRE WITHIN 24 HOURS HE SHOULD BE FINE."

JANET WAS TAKEN BY THE SUCCUBI AND FED UPON - JUST LIKE PETER.

BUT THE BLOODLINE WAS BROKEN - RHYLOS KILLED.

SHE WAKES UP IN THE FINAL ROOM.